Renewals can be made
by internet   www.onfife.com/fife-libraries
in person   at any library in Fife
by phone   03451 55 00 66

ON
AT FIFE
LIBRARIES

Thank you for using your library

Published by Puffin 2013
A Penguin Company
Penguin Books Ltd, 80 Strand, London, WC2R 0RL, UK
Penguin Group (USA) Inc., 375 Hudson Street, New York 10014, USA
Penguin Books Australia Ltd, 707 Collins Street, Melbourne, Victoria 3008,
Australia (A division of Pearson Australia Group Pty Ltd)
Canada, India, New Zealand, South Africa

Written by Cavan Scott
Illustrated by Dani Geremia – Beehive Illustration Agency

www.puffinbooks.co

ISBN: 978-1-40939-2
001
Printed in Great Brit

ALWAYS LEARNING   PEARSON

LIGHTNING ROD
FACES THE
CYCLOPS QUEEN

by Onk Beakman

PUFFIN

CONTENTS

ABOUT THE AUTHOR

Onk Beakman knew he wanted to be a world-famous author from the moment he was hatched. In fact, the book-loving penguin was so keen that he wrote his first novel while still inside his egg (to this day, nobody is entirely sure where he got the tiny pencil and notebook from).

Growing up on the icy wastes of Skylands' Frozen Desert was difficult for a penguin who hated the cold. While his brothers plunged into the freezing waters, Onk could be found with his beak buried in a book and a pen clutched in his flippers.

Yet his life changed forever when a giant floating head appeared in the skies above the tundra. It was Kaos, attempting to melt the icecaps so he could get his grubby little hands on an ancient weapon buried beneath the snow.

Onk watched open-beaked as Spyro swept in and sent the evil Portal Master packing. From that day, Onk knew that he must chronicle the Skylanders' greatest adventures. He travelled the length and breadth of Skylands, collecting every tale he could find about Master Eon's brave champions.

Today, Onk writes from a shack on the beautiful sands of Blistering Beach with his two pet sea cucumbers.

CHAPTER **ONE**

THE STORM TITAN GAMES

"Ladies and gentlemen, we are proud to present the greatest champion Skylands has ever known – Lightning Rod!"

The crowd went wild as soon as Lightning Rod's name was announced. They cheered; they clapped; they threw their hats in the air. A couple of Rotting Robbies even threw their heads in the air, but the less said about that the better. Lightning Rod was the most popular contestant in the annual Storm Titan Games. In fact, some said he was the most popular contestant in the event's entire history. No one had won as many

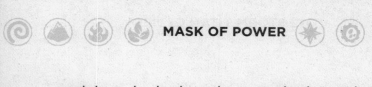

medals as he had, and no one had anywhere near as many statues carved in their image. They were everywhere you looked: Rod throwing a lightning bolt; Rod running a marathon; Rod lifting an entire herd of sabre-tusked elephants stacked on top of each other. There was even a statue of Rod snoring his beard off. Even when asleep, Rod was the most impressive specimen for miles around. No one performed like Rod, no one flexed their

muscles like Rod, and no one polished off as many eggs for breakfast as Rod.

In the crowd, Pop Fizz bounced up and down in his seat as everyone's favourite Storm Titan made his way into the arena.

"Hey, watch it!" said Cali, as the excitable alchemist slopped potion all over her. "You're spilling that stuff everywhere!"

"Whoops, sorry," apologized Pop Fizz, before taking a slug from the bottle. There was a puff of smoke and the distinct whiff of brimstone, and Pop Fizz transformed into a hairy beast with more teeth than was healthy.

"I'm just so pumped up to be here," he rumbled, suddenly taking up twice as much room as he had before his transformation. "Go Lightning! Go Lightning!"

"Stop moving," snapped Drobot from the other side of Pop Fizz. "You are interfering with my visual circuits!"

With a gurgle, Pop Fizz shrank back to his normal size.

"Whoops again," he spluttered, his eyes spinning from the sudden metamorphosis. "This is exciting though, isn't it? I mean, look at this place."

Drobot had to admit that the arena was spectacular. Over a billion Games had been played here, and every year the Storm Titans added on another new stand. It now stretched for miles and seated millions of spectators, all of whom were now looking expectantly at Lightning Rod. The brilliant blue hero stood in the middle of the field, soaking up the

applause, flexing his bulging muscles and flashing a blinding smile.

Cali was grinning too. Rod was in his element here, surrounded by his adoring fans. Yes, she knew that he loved being a Skylander, protecting the magical realm of Skylands from the forces of Darkness, but he was also massively proud of his sporting accomplishments. They all were.

"Do you think he's going to do it?" Pop Fizz asked, half-raising the soda bottle to his lips before being stopped by Drobot. "Do you think he's going to break the record?"

"There is a ninety-nine point nine nine nine per cent probability that Rod will triumph."

"Eh?" said Pop Fizz, looking completely bewildered.

"He said yes," whispered Cali as a hush fell over the crowd.

In the royal box, the King of the Storm Titans had raised his hands. "My friends," he boomed, his voice like a thousand thunderstorms rolled into one. "Please be silent for our guest of honour."

Beside the king stood a tall thin man, leaning heavily on a crystal-topped staff. It was Eon, Skylands' greatest Portal Master. Eon had been asked to open this year's Games, but he looked so old, so tired. Cali frowned. She knew the last few weeks had been a trial for the ancient wizard, but she'd hoped the excitement of the Games would revive him. Still, the Portal Master smiled as he drew himself up, his eyes resting on Lightning Rod far below.

"People of Skylands," Eon said, his voice magically amplified around the stadium. "It is my pleasure to pronounce these Games . . . open."

 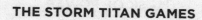
A buzz of excitement rippled around the assembled throng. "And without further ado, we shall enjoy the first event – the five-hundred ton hammer throw. And our first contender, Lightning Rod!"

The crowd roared once again as Lightning Rod approached the massive metal ball and chain at the centre of the field. It was twice the size of the Titan, and yet he grabbed the heavy chain without hesitation. Taking the strain, he began to spin the ball round, faster and faster, electricity crackling up and down the metal links.

Cali couldn't help but be impressed. She often worked with the Skylanders, training them to use their powers, but she'd never seen Lightning Rod lift something this heavy, let alone spin it round.

"He's gonna win," Pop Fizz was babbling, almost beside himself. "He's gonna get the gold. I just know it."

But Drobot didn't comment.

Cali turned and saw he wasn't looking at Lightning Rod, but into the sky.

"What's wrong?" she asked, the fur on the back of her neck bristling.

"That is wrong," Drobot replied, pointing towards the clouds with a claw. Cali turned to see a solitary balloon drifting high above them. "If Lightning Rod lets go of the hammer . . ."

Cali didn't need him to complete the sentence. Worst of all, she knew who owned the balloon.

It was Flynn, the so-called best pilot in all of Skylands, and someone who seemed to have a knack for flying into trouble. The guy had an ego the size of an entire island, but he'd helped the Skylanders time and time again.

"We've got to warn them!" Cali cried out.

"Too late," reported Drobot as the Storm Titan let go of the chain and flung the hammer into the air. It rocketed up, soaring over the heads of the crowd . . . and zoomed straight for Flynn's balloon.

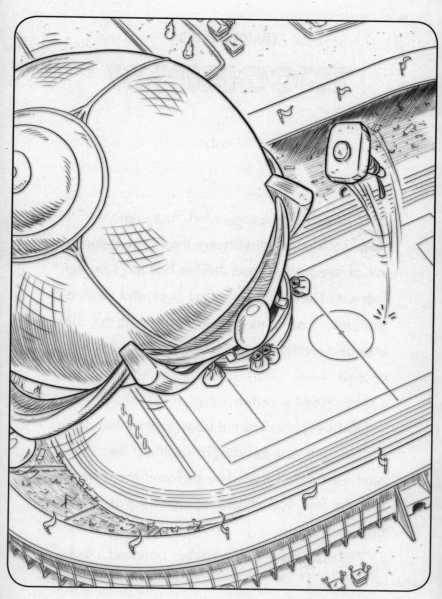

CHAPTER TWO

INCOMING!

Everything happened so fast. Before Cali could shout a warning, the hammer soared out of the stadium and hit the balloon's basket. There was a flash of blinding light and the craft went into a spin, its propeller snapping off. The balloon went one way and the propeller went another.

The crowd gasped.

Drobot calculated the trajectory of the rogue propeller. It was heading straight for one of the many statues of Rod. The balloon, meanwhile, was in free fall, plummeting towards where Eon was sitting.

With a crash, the propeller bounced off the

statue and ricocheted in the direction of the stands.

The crowd screamed.

There was no time to lose. Drobot shot into the air, shouting over his shoulder, "You deal with the propeller. I will stop the balloon!"

The crowd scattered as the whirling blades spun towards them. Beside Cali, Pop Fizz downed an entire bottle of potion and transformed into his fuzzy beast form.

"Let's play ball," he growled, grabbing an empty bench. Just as the propeller was about to plough into the fleeing spectators, Pop Fizz swung the bench like a bat and whacked the blades out of harm's way.

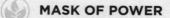

Meanwhile, on the playing field, Lightning Rod had raced over to the royal box. As the balloon came crashing down, the Storm Titan threw himself forward, stretching out his muscular arms to shield Eon and the king.

But the crash never came. At the last moment, Drobot streaked over their heads and grabbed one of the basket's guy-ropes in his jaws. His gyro-gears whirring, the dragon heaved with all his might and pulled the balloon away from the royal box. Back in the stands, Cali gasped. Drobot was moving too quickly; there was no way he'd be able to pull up in time. She saw the dragon fire his retro-thrusters, but it was too late. With the sound of splintering wood and billowing silk, robo-dragon, basket and balloon all smashed into the immaculate turf, sending up a wave of grass and earth.

The crowd fell silent as the balloon deflated over the crash site. Even Lightning Rod clasped a hand over his mouth, fearing the worst. Then

there was a roar of jet engines and Drobot blasted out of the heap of fabric, Flynn dangling from his claws. Everyone burst into applause, whooping and cheering, none more so than Lightning Rod whose clapping sounded like thunder. The Skylanders had saved the day.

Cali, however, didn't join in the celebrations.

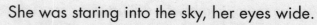

She was staring into the sky, her eyes wide.

"Rod! she yelled. "Look up! Look up!"

Lightning Rod spotted Cali out of the corner of his eye and did as he was told. High above them, the statue the propeller had hit was leaning dangerously. Even worse, a crack was appearing along its neck. The humongous head lolled forward, broke away and plummeted down towards Eon and the king. It was going to squash them alive!

"By my beard and biceps, I shall save them!" exclaimed Rod, tossing a crackling bolt of lightning into the sky. It slammed into the tumbling head, smashing it into a thousand tiny pieces.

"Thank you, Rod," gasped Eon, as dust floated down around him. "I'm sorry about your statue though."

The Storm Titan threw up a hand, shrugging off the apology. "It matters not. They could never get my chin right anyway."

Above them, Flynn was still hanging from the talons of a hovering Drobot. "Woo-hoo!" he cried out as Drobot lowered him to the ground. "What a ride! But don't worry, I'm still in one piece and twice as handsome. BOOM!"

"It's a good thing you weren't carrying any passengers," Eon said, glancing over the crash site. "They could have been really hurt."

Flynn swallowed hard.

"Flynn, you weren't carrying any passengers, were you?" the Portal Master asked, his voice grave.

The pilot laughed nervously.

"Do I look like the kind of guy who forgets about his passengers?"

When no one answered, he turned on his heel and ran towards the middle of the balloon wreckage.

"I'll just check if they're all right!"

CHAPTER THREE
SQUIRMGRUB

"**H**elp!" came a muffled cry from beneath the upturned basket. As Cali and Pop Fizz ran up to join the other Skylanders, Rod grabbed the wicker gondola and flung it aside.

Underneath, a huge robot figure was flailing about on the floor, arms and legs jerking left, right and centre.

"That's a Warrior Librarian," Cali gasped. "But what's wrong with it?"

"It's lying on top of me, that's what's wrong with it!" shouted whoever was still trapped beneath the librarian.

"Allow me," Drobot said, leaning over the twitching cyborg and snapping open a control panel in its side. He plunged a claw inside and started flipping switches. "The crash has caused it to short circuit."

"Can you fix it?" Cali asked.

"Of course," came the sharp reply. "Just rebooting the system and . . ."

The librarian's armour beeped and its legs stopped thrashing. "Repair complete."

"Thank you," the librarian said, finally back in charge of its body. Flexing its mechanical arms, the hulking robot sat up sharply. "I need to talk to Master Eon."

"And I need to breathe!" insisted the voice from beneath it.

The robot gasped, apologized and, taking a welcome hand from Rod, pulled itself up to its large metal feet.

"Hugo!" Cali exclaimed as soon as she realized who had been trapped beneath the bulky armour. "And Double Trouble too. Are you guys OK?"

"We are now," gasped Hugo, Eon's faithful

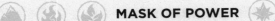
right-hand Mabu. Beside him, Double Trouble was also getting to his feet – or at least he would have been if he had any. Like Rod, Drobot and Pop Fizz, the small but powerful witch doctor was a Skylander, although none of them had ever seen him looking so dishevelled. His feathers were crooked, his Eldritch staff was bent in two and his wooden mask appeared to be on upside down. At least everyone assumed it was a mask. For all they knew it actually was Double Trouble's face.

"Well then," Flynn said cheerfully, clapping his hands together. "All's well that ends well. No harm done, eh?"

"No harm done?" spluttered Hugo, straightening his mangled spectacles. Both lenses had been smashed in the crash. "Look at the state of my glasses. I can't see a thing."

"Calm down, Hugo," said Eon. "That is easily fixed." The Portal Master clicked his fingers, there was a flash of light, and Hugo's glasses were miraculously fixed. Even Double Trouble was back to normal, feathers primped, staff straightened and face the right way round. The tiki-man cheered, firing some test blasts from his Eldritch staff to test it was still working OK (and narrowly missing a passing shoal of flying fish, who scattered in panic).

"Now what is this all about?" Eon asked.

"Master Eon, this is Squirmgrub," Hugo said, indicating the Warrior Librarian that towered over him. "He has discovered something about the Mask of Power."

Eon's face darkened. "Is it news of the next segment?"

Hugo nodded, his newly repaired glasses bouncing on his nose. "Indeed it is. Squirmgrub believes he knows where it can be found."

"The next what?" Cali said, completely bemused. Everyone seemed to know what was happening, but she was still in the dark. "And what's the Mask of Power, anyway?"

The Skylanders explained as Lightning Rod led Eon and the Warrior Librarian to his trophy room deep within the stadium.

"It all started when Kaos tried to steal a book from the Warrior Librarians," Pop Fizz was saying.

Cali felt her hair stand on end at the mention of Kaos. He was the Skylanders' arch-enemy, an evil Portal Master who was always trying to take over Skylands.

"Which book was it?" she asked.

"The Book of Power and Other Utterly Terrifying Stuff," Pop Fizz answered.

"Volume three!" chipped in Hugo, wringing his hands together in worry.

"That doesn't sound like light reading."

"It's not, Cali," Hugo continued. "Not at all. The Book of Power tells of a mysterious artefact from the dark times . . ."

"The Mask of Power, right?"

"The very same, although the ancients knew it by its full name – The Infernal Mask of Malevolent Power, Dominion, Dread and Tyranny."

"I think I prefer the short version," Cali admitted.

"According to legend, the Mask grants its wearer terrible powers."

"Such as?" asked Flynn.

"No one knows for sure," Hugo said, "but they were bad enough for the Portal Masters of old to break the Mask into eight pieces, one for each Element, and scatter them across Skylands."

"And Kaos is trying to find the fragments," Cali guessed.

"Aye. The foul fiend already has one," revealed Rod. "The fragment of Tech. But we hold another."

Hugo nodded. "The Water segment, safe and sound in the Warrior Librarians' Eternal Archive."

"Now all we have to do is find the rest before Kaos does," said Pop Fizz as they finally reached the trophy room.

"Sounds simple enough," said Flynn. "What are we waiting for?"

"It's not that simple," said Hugo. "To stop the Mask from falling into the wrong hands . . ."

"Or on to the wrong face," added Pop Fizz.

". . . the book only reveals the segments one fragment at a time."

They gathered around a table and Cali

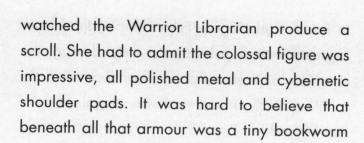
watched the Warrior Librarian produce a scroll. She had to admit the colossal figure was impressive, all polished metal and cybernetic shoulder pads. It was hard to believe that beneath all that armour was a tiny bookworm who could fit comfortably in her palm.

"So, Squirmgrub, what have you to show us?" asked Eon, nodding towards the scroll.

"After you left for the Games," the librarian began, "a picture appeared in the Book of Power. I made a copy." Carefully, he rolled the paper out flat. "I believe it's the Air segment."

Cali noticed Lightning Rod's ears prick up. That made sense. He was an Air Skylander after all. She peered across the table to see what was on the paper.

"But that doesn't look like a piece of mask," said Flynn, scratching his head. "It looks more like a big fish."

"The ancient Portal Masters camouflaged each of the fragments to make them more difficult to find," said Hugo. "For example, the Water segment was disguised as a dirty old rag, the complete opposite of pure, clean water."

"And the Tech segment was disguised as a flower," added Pop Fizz.

"And the Air segment was made to look like a fish?" asked Flynn, still none the wiser.

"Not just any fish," cut in Drobot, who had been checking his database. "Identification confirmed – this creature is a Land Whale."

"Correct," said Hugo, polishing his glasses. "One of the largest and heaviest creatures ever to crawl across the face of Skylands. Although, 'crawl' is a bit of an exaggeration. Land Whales were so heavy they could hardly move."

"Well, it makes sense," said Pop Fizz. "Disguising the Air segment as Skylands' heaviest creature. No one would guess what it actually was."

"But where do you find these Land Whales?"

asked Lightning Rod.

"That's the problem," continued Hugo, popping his specs back on to his nose. "You don't. Land Whales became extinct hundreds of years ago."

"I know where you can find one," said Cali quietly.

"No one's seen one for centuries," insisted Hugo.

"I've seen one," repeated Cali.

"It's a hopeless cause," concluded Hugo. "The Book of Power must be mistaken."

"And you must have forgotten to wash your ears out this morning," exclaimed Pop Fizz, bopping Hugo on the head with one of his potion bottles. "Didn't you just hear Cali?"

"Ow," complained Hugo. "Didn't I hear Cali what?"

"SAY SHE KNOWS WHERE A LAND WHALE IS!" said all of the Skylanders at once.

"Oh," said Hugo, rubbing his head.

"Where did you see a Land Whale, Cali?" asked Eon gently.

Cali blushed as all eyes turned towards her.

"Well, it was back in the days before I met you guys, when I explored Skylands. I was blown off course and stumbled across Tempest Towers, a city ruled by a family of cyclopses. The Cyclops Queen had the most amazing zoo. There were hippo-sized butterflies, double-headed swans and . . ."

"A Land Whale?" prompted Lightning Rod.

Cali nodded. "According to the queen it was the last of its kind."

"It must be the Air segment in disguise," said Pop Fizz, bouncing up and down. "We just need to go to Tempest Towers to check. Easy."

"I wouldn't be so sure," Eon warned. "The Tempest Tower itself is carved from pure Cyclopnite."

"From pure what?"

"The heaviest, densest and strongest stone

ever mined," Hugo explained. "The walls of the city and the queen's menagerie are said to be the thickest in all of Skylands."

"Then I shall merely knock them down," announced Rod, as confident as ever.

"That is quite impossible," said Eon sadly. "Even for you, old friend. No. You will not be able to fight your way into the queen's collection. This mission calls for stealth and cunning. You will have to use your brains to find the whale, not your brawn."

"There is another snag," admitted Cali. "Tempest Towers lies beyond the Sea of Storms."

"That doesn't sound so bad," said Flynn. "What's the Sea of Storms anyway?"

"Only the most dangerous stretch of sky in all of Skylands," answered Eon with a sigh. "An expanse of turbulent tornados, hideous hurricanes and horrific hailstorms."

"Not to mention all those Windbag Djinnis," added Hugo. "Evil living clouds that will blow you out of the sky as soon as look at you. It's so treacherous there that not even Master Eon can send a Portal through the storms. The only way to get through is by airship or balloon."

"OK," said a distinctly crestfallen Pop Fizz. "Suddenly all this doesn't sound so easy after all."

"Indeed," sniffed Hugo. "It's certain doom for anyone who even tries to sail through the Sea of Storms."

"Ha! Certain doom for anyone who isn't Skylands' greatest pilot," insisted Flynn, wiggling his eyebrows at Cali. "When do we leave?"

CHAPTER FOUR

At first, Lightning Rod had been a little miffed that he would miss the rest of the Storm Titan Games. Of course, he claimed he was only thinking of his fans. How would they cope without seeing him win another gold medal?

Eon, as wise as ever, soon talked the Skylander round. Who better to help navigate the Sea of Storms than a Storm Titan? And not just any Storm Titan at that – the greatest Storm Titan who had ever lived.

"Come now," Lightning Rod said, his expansive chest puffing up with pride. "I am sure the others would rise to the challenge." Rod paused, as if considering it. "Although, no one knows as much about storms as Lightning Rod."

"And you have completed plenty of quests in your time," added Cali.

"Indeed, noble Cali," Rod agreed. "Hundreds."

Eon just rested on his staff, waiting for Rod's not inconsiderable ego to do the convincing.

"In fact," Rod continued, rising ever so slightly into the air, "I can think of no one better for the task than Lightning Rod, champion of the Cloud Kingdom."

Cali shared a secret smile with the Portal Master. Lightning Rod was their friend, and a powerful ally to be able to call upon, but he did love himself at times. She supposed it wasn't really his fault. It must be hard to be humble when you're surrounded by all those statues of yourself.

Still, Cali was pleased that Lightning Rod was going with them. Drobot had done a great job patching up the basket and rebuilding the propeller, but the journey ahead was going to be a difficult one. It wasn't that she didn't think

Flynn could make it. Despite the odd mishap, the big lug was a brilliant pilot, although she'd never admit it to his face. But could he make it through the Sea of Storms? Her last journey to Tempest Towers had been hair-raising enough, and she'd only just made it through in one piece.

Eon handed the Storm Titan a scrap of paper. "This is from the Book of Power," he explained. "It will glow when you get near the Air segment. Good luck in your quest."

"Luck?" bellowed Rod, tucking the paper into his cloud. "I've never needed luck. Do not fear. This will be my greatest triumph!"

High above them, lightning flashed in time with Rod's voice.

"Whoops, looks like rain," said a voice behind them. "Coming through. Excuse me."

Cali turned round to see Pop Fizz struggling across the arena with dozens of bottles in his arms. The moment Eon had asked them to go to Tempest Towers, the alchemist had rushed off to whip up another batch of magic potion. How much did he think he'd need? With a giggle, she noticed another figure following close behind. It was Double Trouble, carrying yet more bottles and muttering under his breath in his strange language. "Mooga booga dooga vooga."

"I'm inclined to agree," said Eon, demonstrating his impressive understanding of the Ooga tongue. "All those bottles may be too heavy for Flynn's balloon."

"It will never leave the ground," insisted Rod.

"It's OK," Pop Fizz replied. "I'll just drink them and . . . whoa!"

A bottle slipped from the top of Pop Fizz's pile and tumbled under his feet. The alchemist slipped and fell, bottles flying everywhere. Cali threw up her hands, expecting to be smothered in potion, but Double Trouble had already jumped into action.

"Booga-boo!" he cried out, summoning three miniature duplicates of himself. The clones scampered forward, nimbly catching the falling bottles and throwing them back into Pop Fizz's arms, before charging to grab the next. Then, as quickly as they appeared, the tiny doubles vanished, harmlessly exploding into tiny puffs of smoke.

"Th-thanks," stammered Pop Fizz, still a little in shock. "You're one in a million. Or should that be four in a million?"

Double Trouble beamed, his mood instantly lifted. He bustled past Cali, humming a little song to himself as he weaved over to the balloon.

"Are you coming, Cali?" Pop Fizz asked,

carefully watching the pile of bottles to make sure another didn't drop. "I think Flynn's ready to get going."

But Cali wasn't listening. She'd spotted something, over by the stands. A Mabu child was sitting by herself and it looked like she was crying.

"Cali?" Pop Fizz repeated.

"What? Oh, yes, I'll be right over. You go ahead."

Pop Fizz shrugged and carried on. Cali, meanwhile, jogged over to the crying girl. Perhaps her family had left her behind after the crowds had headed home.

"Hey honey, are you all right?" she asked, leaning forward and touching the young Mabu's arm.

The infant sniffed, wiped her nose with the back of her hand and looked up at Cali with wide, teary eyes.

Wide teary eyes that were glowing green! That wasn't right. Before Cali could react, the

Mabu's tiny paw shot up and grabbed her wrist. Grabbed it tight.

"Oh, everything is all right now," the Mabu hissed, but it wasn't the voice of a Mabu at all. It was an evil, twisted voice – a voice that wouldn't have sounded out of place in the middle of a nightmare.

Cali tried to pull away, but the Mabu's grip was like a vice. Cali struggled, shouting out, but was caught fast.

"Going somewhere?" came another voice from above. Cali looked up to see a massive airship shimmer into view above the stadium. A Drow zeppelin, its deck lined with legions of heavily armed dark elves. As she watched, a face peered over the side of the ship, a sickening grin stretching from one evil ear to the other.

Kaos!

"Do you have her?" the villainous Portal Master yelled down. Beside Cali, the impossibly strong Mabu nodded.

"I do, Lord Kaos," the child replied, before its body seemed to blur, to grow. Suddenly, it wasn't a young Mabu that held Cali by the wrist at all. It was a Drow Witch. "I have the explorer."

"Then what are you waiting for? Bring her to me! Bring her to me NOOOW!"

"At once, Lord Kaos," the witch called back, and began to float up towards the airship, dragging Cali with her.

The Skylanders hadn't noticed the sudden appearance of the Drow zeppelin. They had been too busy trying to stow Pop Fizz's excessive supplies of potion into Flynn's wicker basket. But they didn't miss Cali's scream.

Lightning Rod span round and immediately sprang into action, roaring Cali's name. He drew his arm back, preparing to fire an electric bolt at the zeppelin's balloon, when a boom reverberated round the stadium.

"Look out," Eon cried, but it was too late. A

cannonball smacked into Rod's chest, knocking him on to his back. Annoyed, Rod brushed the heavy iron ball away as easily as if he were swatting a fly, before looking up to see more missiles screaming towards them.

Eon stepped forward, shouting an ancient incantation. The air around them shimmered and, with a resounding clang, the cannonballs clattered off the magical forcefield the Portal Master had summoned. Lightning Rod found himself surrounded by his fellow Skylanders as they checked he was OK. He angrily brushed them away.

Of course he wasn't OK! He'd never been so humiliated in his life. Knocked on to his back in the middle of his own home stadium? Not to mention the fact that one of his closest friends had just been taken captive right under his, admittedly splendid, nose. Someone would pay for this. Kaos would pay.

"Come back, coward!" the Storm Titan yelled.

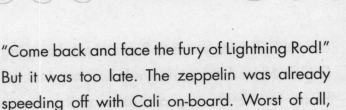

"Come back and face the fury of Lightning Rod!"
But it was too late. The zeppelin was already
speeding off with Cali on-board. Worst of all,
they could hear Kaos' mocking laughter even
over the sound of its engine.

"Bye-bye, Skyblunderers. It's been nice
BEATING YOU!"

"That creep's got Cali!" shouted Flynn,
frantically preparing his balloon for emergency
take-off. "Poor gal is probably missing me
already."

Flynn wasn't fooling anyone. Even through his
usual bluster, it was obvious that he was beside
himself with worry. Everyone knew he adored her.

"But why would he take Cali?" Pop Fizz asked,
scrambling into the basket.

"It is obvious," rumbled Lightning Rod, already
thundering after the zeppelin. "Kaos must have
heard that only Cali knows the path to Tempest
Towers."

"But how?" asked Pop Fizz to an equally

confused-looking Double Trouble. The tiki-man didn't get a chance to reply as the balloon lurched into the sky.

"Up, up, and away!" yelled Flynn, the propeller whirring furiously. "Let's go save the babe!"

CHAPTER FIVE

BATTLE STATIONS!

"**U**gh! This is no way to travel," Kaos moaned.

On the Drow ship, a Goliath Drow was tying Cali to the central mast, the coarse rope rubbing painfully against her arms. The zeppelin lurched to the left and Kaos turned almost as green as his Drow minions.

"What is wrong with that fool of a captain?" Kaos griped, steadying himself against the side of the boat. "Can't he keep this bucket of bolts steady?"

"He's doing the best he can, Lord Kaos," said

a lanky troll. It was Glumshanks, the sickly Portal Master's long-suffering sidekick.

"Not good enough! THROW THE FOOL OVERBOARD!" Kaos shrieked. The Portal Master pointed at the Goliath Drow. "You! What's your name?"

"Brock," came the nervous reply.

"Wrong!" Kaos shrieked. "It's Captain Brock! This is your ship now. Take the wheel."

The Drow broke into a toothy grin. "Brock is captain?" he queried.

"That's what I said, isn't it?"

"Brock won't let you down. Brock will be the best captain in history. Brock . . ."

". . . will also be thrown overboard if he doesn't take the wheel RIGHT THIS MINUTE!" Kaos yelled.

Brock did what he was told.

Sighing, Kaos lowered himself on to a barrel. "I hate boats almost as much as I hate trees," he groaned, clutching his stomach. "Those leafy

louts have it in for me. When I, KAOS, am lord of all, all trees will be DOOOOMED!!"

Cali let out a snort of laughter and was rewarded with a withering glare.

"What are you sniggering at, FOOL?"

"Oh, just the thought of you being 'lord of all'," she chuckled. "You don't stand a chance."

"Shows how much you know," Kaos snapped. "Everything has been planned to the smallest detail. Here, I shall show you!"

With that, Kaos started rooting around in his robe. "Where is it?" he screamed. "Glumshanks! Where is the plan?"

"The plan, master?" Glumshanks replied cautiously. "Do you mean the plan for complete and utter universal domination?"

"Yes, I mean the plan for complete and utter universal domination. The plan I spent months working on. The plan that we were not to forget to bring under any circumstances."

"Perhaps you forgot to bring it, sir?"

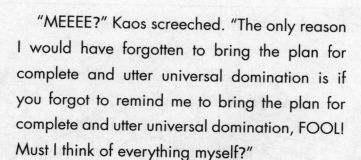

"MEEEE?" Kaos screeched. "The only reason I would have forgotten to bring the plan for complete and utter universal domination is if you forgot to remind me to bring the plan for complete and utter universal domination, FOOL! Must I think of everything myself?"

Giving Cali a tired look, Glumshanks reached into his back pocket and produced a small, battered notebook. "Sorry master," he apologized, even though it was obviously not his fault. "Luckily I made a copy, in case you forgot . . ."

"WHHHHHHAT?"

"I-I mean, in case I forgot to remind you not to forget to bring it with us."

Muttering about being surrounded by amateurs, Kaos snatched the book and started flicking through its dog-eared pages. He then cleared his throat and began to read out loud.

"Step one: kidnap Cali." He gave the explorer an evil smirk. "Done!"

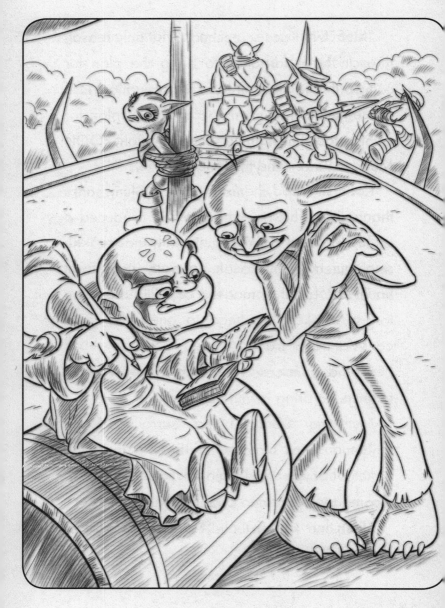

"Step two: force Cali to navigate our way through the Sea of Storms.

Step three: grab the Land Whale, A.K.A. the Air segment.

Step four: find all the other fragments of the Mask of Power and become LORD OF ALL!"

Kaos snapped the book shut, looking more than a little pleased with himself.

"Sooo, what do you think of that? Granted, step four needs a little more work, but I think you'll agree that victory will be MIIINE!"

Cali cocked her head to one side, as if considering it for a minute. Then she shook her head. "Nah. Still don't think you stand a chance."

"And why is that?"

"Because we're about to be boarded by a bunch of Skylanders," said Glumshanks glumly, looking over the side of the ship.

"Exactly!" said Cali, with a knowing smile.

"NOOOOOOOO!" Kaos screamed,

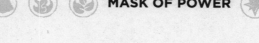
spinning round. His eyes widened as he saw Flynn's balloon in hot pursuit.

"Battle stations!" yelled Flynn, getting into the spirit of the occasion. Beside him, Pop Fizz was already downing potion by the bottle-load, while Double Trouble summoned a host of explosive clones. The basket was getting more than a little crowded.

"Target in range," reported Drobot, his wing lasers charged and ready to fire.

"Then what are we waiting for?" bellowed Lightning Rod. "Prepare to feel my wrath, evil ones."

He drew his arm back and tossed a ball of crackling electricity at the zeppelin.

The bolt smashed into the deck by Kaos' feet. The wicked Portal Master shrieked and jumped up on his barrel as if he'd just seen a mouse. Laser-fire streaked through the air as Drobot swooped by.

"They're attacking, sir!" shouted Brock from the ship's wheel.

Another bolt blasted through the hull of the ship.

"Oh, really?" Kaos sneered sarcastically. "I hadn't noticed! DO SOMETHING ABOUT IT, FOOL! BLOW THEM OUT OF THE SKY!!!"

On the balloon, Pop Fizz had drunk so much potion he was twice his normal size.

"Ooga," said Double Trouble, conjuring up a mini-clone of himself. "Throw-ga booga."

"Hey, I understood that!" shouted Flynn. "He wants you to chuck it at them. Maybe I'm getting the hang of this."

Fizz picked up the tiny tiki-man and chucked it on-board the zeppelin. A second later, they heard it explode.

"Another, another," Pop Fizz babbled as Drobot swooped back to join them.

"Cali is tied to the main mast," the dragon

reported. "We need more speed."

"We're going as fast as we can," Flynn insisted, pumping the controls furiously. "The engine won't take much more."

"Keep going!" Lightning Rod shouted, letting loose another barrage of crackling bolts. "We're nearly on them!"

"They're nearly on us!" screamed Kaos as a Double Trouble clone bounced off his head and detonated. "Where are those cannons?"

"It's no good," Glumshanks yelled. "The Skylanders are too fast. The cannons can't lock on to them."

"Who said we were aiming at the Skylanders?" Kaos called back.

All along the hull of the zeppelin, portholes clattered open.

"Observation," said Drobot, dryly. "They're preparing the cannons."

Sure enough, hulking guns appeared in the gaps, facing straight towards them.

Remembering the cannonball back at the arena, Rod immediately put himself between the guns and Flynn's balloon. The Drow had been lucky with their first shot. This time would be different.

BOOM! The first cannon fired, but the cannonball zoomed wide of the Storm Titan.

"Ha!" he bellowed. "Missed!"

BANG! Another cannon fired. Rod watched the cannonball shriek past Drobot and narrowly miss the balloon.

Suddenly, Lightning Rod realized what was happening.

"No!" he cried out. "They are aiming at the balloon. They mean to burst it!"

Cali watched in horror while Flynn's balloon bobbed left and right as the pilot tried to evade the cannonballs. "Stop it!" she yelled. "You'll hit Flynn!"

"Ha!" snorted Kaos. "That's the idea, FOOL! Pop that balloon! Send them to their DOOOOOOOM!"

"You're evil," Cali spat, straining at her bonds. "Absolutely evil."

Kaos gasped and batted his eyelashes at her in mock surprise.

"Oh, Cali, you say the nicest things. Bwa-ha-ha-haaaaaaaa!"

"We must protect the balloon!" Lightning Rod commanded as the guns fired again. If the balloon were hit, the basket containing the pilot, Double Trouble and Pop Fizz would drop like a stone. Drobot flew ahead, managing to deflect a couple of cannonballs with a timely laser blast, but he couldn't destroy them all.

A cannonball came screaming through the air, straight towards Lightning Rod. The Storm Titan twisted round and punched it away with a grunt. He did the same with the next, and the one after that.

"Wow-wow-wow-wow!" cheered Pop-Fizz, now chucking three potion bottles at a time.

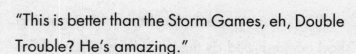

"This is better than the Storm Games, eh, Double Trouble? He's amazing."

But Double Trouble didn't answer.

On the Drow ship, Kaos clapped his hands together with glee. His plan was working. The Skylanders were so busy trying to block the cannonballs that they'd stopped attacking the zeppelin altogether.

"That's it, Brock. That's it! While the Skylosers are busy, FULL SPEED AHEAD!"

"Aye-aye," Brock yelled back. "Engine room. Give Brock all you've got."

Lightning Rod was having the time of his life. The cannonballs were coming faster than ever, but he could do this all day.

Three more cannonballs shot towards the Storm Titan and he took them out. One. Two. Three.

"I am invincible!" he cried out in victory, just as he heard a cry from the balloon.

"Rod! Rod!" yelled Pop Fizz. "There's something wrong with Double Trouble!"

CHAPTER SIX

THE WINDBAG DJINNIS

"They're getting away!" called out Drobot as Lightning Rod flew back to the balloon. The dragon was right, but Rod had other concerns. In the basket, Double Trouble was standing stock still, rigid arms holding his staff aloft and his eyes screwed tight. Even the paintwork of his mask had changed. The colours looked darker, as if the tiki-man was holding his breath.

"What in my name is he doing?" Rod asked, scratching his beard.

"One minute he's blasting out doubles,"

Flynn added, "and the next – KA-BLAMMO! He makes like a statue!"

With a roar of jet engines, Drobot circled the balloon and came to rest on the edge of the wicker basket. "My sensors indicate Double Trouble is in a trance," the dragon reported.

"This is no time to take a nap," insisted Flynn. "The bad guys have skedaddled with Cali."

"Mooga . . ." hissed a low, controlled voice. "Ooga . . . sooga . . ."

"Double Trouble!" exclaimed Pop Fizz. "He can hear us!"

Lightning Rod peered in closer. "I think not. He is still entranced."

"But did you hear what he said?" asked Pop Fizz. "Cali is safe."

"How does he know?" asked a confused Flynn, as Double Trouble spat words through fiercely gritted teeth.

"Oooga . . . booga . . . zooga . . . mooga."

"Incredible," gasped Pop Fizz.

"Yes, I suppose I am," said Flynn, misunderstanding completely. "But what did he say?"

"One of Double Trouble's doubles is still on the zeppelin," Pop Fizz translated. "Somehow he's still seeing through its eyes."

"Usually Double Trouble's clones explode within minutes," Drobot said. "For him to keep one from detonating must be exhausting every ounce of his energy."

"Can his double get to poor Cali?" Flynn asked.

"No, it's hidden," said Pop Fizz, "and can only observe. But she is safe . . . for now. The zeppelin has entered the Sea of Storms. Kaos is forcing her to guide them through the clouds. Double can guide us through."

"Wow," said Flynn. "You got all that from a couple of words. I'm impressed. That must be how you guys feel when you're around me!"

The balloon bucked suddenly. Rod looked

up, his bushy eyebrows creasing into a frown.

"Behold," he boomed, pointing forward with a muscle-bound arm. "The Sea of Storms!"

They all did as they were told, and then wished they hadn't. They were racing towards the largest storm any of them had ever seen, a black swirling cloud stretching as far as the eye could see. Lightning flashed and crackled through the rain, illuminating thousands of smaller clouds swarming towards them.

Rod glared at the sight. They were Windbag Djinnis. In his youth he'd used them as target practice, blasting them out of the sky with lightning bolts. To Storm Titans, Windbags were normally considered to be little more than annoying bugs that were there to be swatted.

But these Windbags were different. They were double the size, and looked twice as nasty. Already, he could see them preparing to batter the balloon with gale-force winds and fry the Skylanders with their electro-blasts.

"Eon wasn't joking when he said it was bad, was he?" said Pop Fizz, his ears pricking up as he prepared himself for the worst.

Lightning Rod clapped his hands together in anticipation. "Victory shall rain down on us, mark my words."

"Yeah," grinned Pop Fizz, new bottles already in hand. "A little rain never hurt anyone, after all!"

"That's the spirit," declared Flynn, yanking back on a big red lever. "With Skylands' greatest pilot at the helm, there's nothing to fear. Although, I would fasten your seat belts. This is going to get bumpy . . ."

"Seat belts?" Pop Fizz asked, looking frantically around the basket. "What seat belts?"

"Oh yeah," Flynn remembered. "Never bothered to get them fitted. Let's go!"

The balloon flew headlong directly into the heart of the Sea of Storms.

CHAPTER SEVEN

THE SEA OF STORMS

Gale-force winds hit them the moment they ploughed into the stormy skies. Rain seemed to pummel them from every direction at once, plastering their hair against their skin and stinging their eyes.

"Observation," called out Drobot. "Windbag Djinnis attacking."

"No kidding!" Pop Fizz yelled back, preparing to launch a volley of potion bottles. "They're everywhere!"

Indeed they were. They also outnumbered the Skylanders a thousand to one. No sooner

had Rod taken out a Windbag with a lightning bolt, than three more appeared in its place.

CRACKLE. Electricity arched across the balloon.

CREAK. The basket groaned in the wind.

SNAP. A piece of the propeller broke off.

"Don't worry!" shouted Flynn. "That's supposed to happen!"

"Sure it is," replied Pop Fizz, frantically shaking a bottle filled with explosive potion. "We'll worry about the storm, you just listen to Double Trouble."

"Listen to him?" Flynn complained. "I can't understand a word that fella says."

"It's simple," Pop Fizz yelled back. "If he says 'ooga', swing the balloon right."

"And what will he say if he wants me to swing the balloon left?"

"'Ooga', probably!"

"Thanks," said Flynn, throwing a control. "That's a big help."

In front of them Rod snapped his fingers, an idea occuring to him. "Of course," he boomed. "That is how I shall defeat them!"

"Care to share the plan, big man?" Flynn squeaked, narrowly avoiding being tossed out of the basket. But Rod didn't answer. He was already rising majestically from the balloon, his arms stretched wide.

"LIGHTNING," he commanded at the top of his voice. "TO ME!!"

The bellow was so loud that it almost drowned out the storm. Electricity burst from the Djinnis, sizzling towards the balloon. The lightning slammed into Rod's outstretched hands, flowing up his arms and over his chest. As he drained every Windbag in the sky, the Storm Titan's hair stood on end, sparks flying from his beard.

"Ha, ha," he laughed, his eyes flashing wildly. "That tickles!"

"You're doing it!" shouted Pop Fizz.

"Of course I am. Look!"

All around them, the Djinnis were blinking out of existence, vanishing one by one as their energy was drained.

"Warning!" said Drobot, his mechanical voice full of concern. "You are absorbing too much power."

"NEVER!" roared Rod. "I just need to release it."

"Release it?" said Flynn, his usual smile faltering. "Won't that be kind of bad for us?"

Drobot's eyes grew wide as another idea popped into his head.

"Not necessarily." The dragon stretched out his wings, revealing the power pack mounted on his back. "Rod, dump the excess energy into my armour."

Rod scowled, every muscle in his neck looking ready to burst. "No. It will be too much for you, heroic dragon."

Drobot shook his head. "I will be able to take it." The dragon was already making adjustments to a control panel on the side of his helmet. "I will divert the extra power to my afterburners and —"

Rod didn't wait for Drobot to finish his sentence. He spun round, slapping a massive palm on to the dragon's power pack. There was a blinding flash of light and the power of over one thousand Windbags jumped across into Drobot's armour.

For a minute it looked like Rod had been right. Drobot's eyes flared as electricity crackled along his wings.

WHOOSH! The dragon's afterburners blasted a column of fire out behind them. Even Lightning Rod screamed as the balloon shot forward at an unbelievable speed.

On the Drow zeppelin, Kaos was not a well Portal Master. If he'd been feeling sky-sick before they hit the Sea of Storms, he felt like death now that they were being tossed back and forth by the ferocious winds.

"Please tell me we're nearly there," he moaned, holding on to the side of the ship for dear life.

"I wish I could," hissed Cali. She knew it would still be some while before they were clear of the storms. "Bear left at the next tornado."

"Brock hears ya!" came a bellow from the steering wheel. Amazingly, the Goliath Drow seemed to be enjoying himself.

"I'm sure it'll be over soon," Glumshanks said, rubbing his master's back to make him feel better.

"Get off me, fool!" Kaos barked, swatting the troll away before groaning as the deck lurched violently.

"At least we're way ahead of those Skyblunderers," burped Kaos, clutching his churning belly. "They'll never catch up with us now."

Beside him, Glumshanks let out a little whimper.

"What is it now?" Kaos snapped. "The trouble

with you is that you're always moaning about something, Glumshanks."

"Remember what you said about the Skylanders? About how they'll never catch up with us?"

"Of course I remember. I've only just said it, fool."

Glumshanks shook his head sadly. His master wasn't going to like this.

"You'd better hold on tight . . ."

"Why? Stop talking in riddles you blundering . . . AAAAAAAARGH!"

Kaos was thrown across the deck as Flynn's balloon rocketed by, nearly knocking the zeppelin from the sky.

"I don't believe it!" shrieked Kaos as the Skylanders' craft disappeared from view. "BROCK, FLY FAAAAAASTER!"

Flynn's balloon barrelled out of the Sea of Storms, Drobot's afterburners still blazing. In the basket, it was all they could do to hang on.

"OK, Drobot," shouted Flynn. "You can stop now, buddy."

"Negative," the robo-dragon replied. "Afterburners not responding. Controls have fused!"

"They'll do more than fuse in a minute," yelled Pop Fizz, pointing ahead. "I'm guessing that large and very solid-looking castle is Tempest Towers."

"Affirmative," said Drobot.

"Anyone know the chances of us stopping before we smash into its walls?" asked Flynn.

"Approximately zero point zero zero one per cent," said Drobot.

"And the odds of us surviving the crash?" the pilot queried.

"Considerably slimmer."

"Thanks for clearing that up," whimpered Flynn. "Now, if it's all right with everyone, I might start screaming. WAAAAAAAH!!"

The walls of Tempest Towers raced towards them.

CHAPTER EIGHT

TEMPEST TOWERS

"**R**erouting controls," reported Drobot, his afterburners still going at full pelt. "Shutting down propulsion systems. Extinguishing rockets in five, four, three –"

"Forget the countdown," yelled Pop Fizz, never taking his eyes off the castle walls. "Do it now, do it now!"

"One!"

The Skylanders cheered as the roaring afterburners finally cut out, although the celebrations soon dwindled when they realized they hadn't slowed down in the slightest.

"Shouldn't we have stopped?" Flynn all but squeaked.

"It's the momentum," Drobot said matter-of-factly. "It's carrying us forward."

"So we're going to crash anyway?"

"Not if I can do anything about it!" Lightning Rod leapt from the basket and, grabbing the ropes, pulled back as hard as he could. The muscles on Rod's shoulders bunched and Pop Fizz closed his eyes, fearing the worst.

WHUMPH!

With a bone-shuddering jolt, the basket came to a halt. Pop Fizz found himself tumbling head over heels. He didn't open his eyes again until he'd come to a halt.

Yes!

They hadn't crashed. Well, not into the walls at least. The basket had ploughed into the strip of rocky ground that surrounded Tempest Towers. They were battered and bruised, but still in the land of the living.

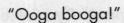

"Ooga booga!"

Pop Fizz spun around to see Double Trouble beside him, eyes wide open with surprise. "Double Trouble, you're out of your trance! Good to have you back, buddy!"

Double Trouble looked around at the chaos surrounding them. "Booga oog?"

"Don't worry," Pop Fizz sniggered, brushing himself down. "You didn't miss anything . . . much."

Meanwhile, in the gatehouse of Tempest Towers, two cyclops guards were playing Skystones. They should, of course, have been watching the gates, but there didn't seem much point. After all, no one ever visited Tempest Towers. If the prospect of crossing the Sea of Storms didn't put people off, the smell definitely did.

It's a sad fact that cyclopses are the smelliest creatures in all of Skylands. Just one sniff of a cyclops can put you off your dinner. The reek of an entire city of the things is enough to make sure you never want to eat again.

Cyclopses, however, are blissfully unaware of their own foul odour as they are born without noses.

Of course, the guards of the gatehouse didn't mind the lack of visitors. The fact that no one had knocked on their gates for more than a decade meant that they had become exceptionally good at Skystones.

"Ha!" shouted the first guard, a spiky-haired Mohawk by the name of Quick Draw. "Level three Bonecrusher! I win!"

"Not again," sighed his opponent, a chubby cyclops known as Slow Hand. "Best out of five thousand?"

A loud bang echoed round the gatehouse.

Slow Hand dropped his Skystones. "What was that?"

"I have no idea," replied Quick Draw.

Another bang rattled the glass in the gatehouse windows.

"It sounds like someone banging on the gate," Slow Hand said in amazement.

"Never!" said Quick Draw.

The two cyclopses ran to the windows. Throwing them open, they peered down to see four strangers standing in front of the gates. The largest, a big blue hulk of a fellow, was about to smash his fist into the wood once again.

"What d'ya want?" shouted Quick Draw.

The strangers looked up and the blue one broke into a dazzling smile.

"Greetings!" he boomed. "We wish to enter your fine city."

Quick Draw and Slow Hand exchanged confused glances.

"Why?" Slow Hand asked.

"Because we desire an audience with your gracious queen."

"And why would she want to see you?" asked Quick Draw.

The blue one laughed, as if he'd never been asked such a thing.

"Why? Because I'm Lightning Rod, of course."

"Who?"

"Lightning Rod. Champion of the Cloud Kingdom. Master of Lightning. Winner of the mightiest beard ten years running. You have heard of me, yes?"

"No," replied Slow Hand.

This Lightning Rod fellow put his hands on his

hips, looking more than a little peeved. "But I'm a Storm Titan. And a Skylander too."

"Oooooh, a Storm Titan," repeated Quick Draw.

"And a Skylander," added Slow Hand, much to the stranger's obvious delight. "Why didn't you say so?"

"So you'll let us in then?"

"No," snapped Slow Hand.

"No?"

"Storm Titans are two-a-penny," said Quick Draw. "And as for Skylanders? Well, there are dozens of you, aren't there?"

"But . . ."

"No buts. The queen only lets unique specimens through her gates. Creatures she's never seen before."

"Look, you one-eyed dolt, all we require is . . ."

The cyclopses didn't let Lightning Rod finish.

"Go away!" they shouted in unison, and slammed their windows shut.

"Well, that's never happened before," said Lightning Rod, utterly mystified.

"So what now?" asked Pop Fizz.

"Observation: it takes one bottle of potion to transform you into your beast form, correct?" enquired Drobot.

"Sure does," said Pop, whipping a bottle out of his satchel.

"What would happen if you drank fifty bottles?"

"Fifty?" Rod spluttered. "Have you gone mad?"

"Do it," Drobot commanded. "Flynn, gather the ropes from the balloon."

The alchemist didn't wait to be asked twice. He started knocking back bottles two at a time, immediately transforming into his hairy form.

"Booga mooga dooga," exclaimed Double Trouble, suddenly realizing what Drobot was planning.

"Right – use the ropes to get him under control, and let's try those gates again," insisted Drobot.

"What now?" yelled Slow Hand, swinging open the window. "I'm trying to win a –"

The sight below made him stop mid-sentence.

"Quick Draw, come and look at this."

His mohawked companion joined him at the window.

"No way!"

"Yes way!" yelled up one of the strangers from below, the one who looked like an armoured dragon. "I can guarantee that your queen has never seen a creature like this before."

The dragon could be right. The one who had called himself Lightning Rod had a blue fuzzy monstrosity tied up by its wrists. The crazed beast was snarling and leaping about, almost pulling the Storm Titan off his cloud.

"He might be right," commented Quick Draw. "That's something you don't see every day."

"Shall we let them in then?"

"Well, if we do, we can get back to our game. Unless you're scared I'll win again?"

The giant gates of Tempest Towers swung open.

"Success!" exclaimed Drobot.

"Yeah, yeah, yeah," babbled the hyperactive beast that used to be Pop Fizz. "Success, success, success."

"So let me get this right," said Flynn. "You take the furball to see the queen and then what? Try to steal this Land Whale thingy when she's not looking?"

"Indeed," Lightning Rod said, straining to keep Pop Fizz on his leash. "A simple task, I am sure."

"You two stay here and keep a look out for Kaos," added Drobot, gesturing to Flynn and Double Trouble as he stepped across the threshold to the castle. "He can't be far behind."

"Is he?" Flynn asked Double Trouble, but the spellcaster just shrugged.

"Booga weh!"

"And I've got no idea what you just said."

"He said that his link to our nemesis has been lost," explained Rod. "Double Trouble's double detonated as soon as he came out of his trance. We no longer have a spy on the Drow craft."

"You got all that from 'booga weh'?"

"Double Trouble is a tiki-man of few words," Lightning Rod said, smiling at his friend, before his expression darkened. "But now we must make haste. Come. We have no time to lose."

"But what do I do when baldie gets here?"

asked an increasingly worried-looking Flynn.

"Just stop him," grunted Lightning Rod, dragging the demented Pop Fizz through the already closing gates.

The doors clanged shut.

"Just stop him," repeated Flynn, anxiously watching the skies. "Just stop a crazy Portal Master and his ship full of heavily armoured Drow."

The pilot turned to Double Trouble and was dismayed to see the tiki-man had started to perform a jaunty war-dance to prepare himself for battle.

"No problem at all," Flynn whimpered.

CHAPTER NINE

THE CYCLOPS QUEEN

By the time Lightning Rod had dragged the snarling alchemist through the streets of Tempest Towers, a crowd of cyclopses had gathered to see the new arrivals.

"Where are we going, dragon?" the Storm Titan whispered to Drobot.

The dragon pointed towards the tower that rose into the sky from the centre of the city.

"That tower is the largest building. Logic dictates that it must be the most important. Plus, the king and queen are sitting in front of its gates."

Sure enough, two thrones were set in front

of the doors of the tower, although it had to be said that the king wasn't exactly an impressive sight. A single, watery eye peered out from beneath a massive crown and the ruler was so tiny that his feet didn't even reach the floor.

The queen, however, was something else.

She was possibly the most hideous creature Rod had ever seen, as wide as her husband was small, with coarse hair erupting from her chin. Yellow, jagged teeth jutted along slack jaws and her bloodshot eyes – all three of them – boggled at Pop Fizz. Rod had to admit that having three eyes was certainly unusual. True to their name, most cyclopses had just one eye, although two-eyed examples weren't unheard of. But three? Perhaps that's why she was so fascinated by unique life-forms; she was pretty unique herself.

"What a wonderful specimen!" she slobbered, clapping her horrible hands together.

"Why, thank you, madam," Rod grinned

and bowed, despite his disgust.

"I think she means Pop Fizz," pointed out Drobot.

"Oh," said Rod, disappointed.

"Fantastic," whined the king, his thin, nasally voice sounding like nails scraping down a blackboard. "Another beast for the menagerie. I can feel my sinuses swelling already."

"Don't mind him," the queen lisped, elbowing her husband so hard his crown slipped over his eye. "He's allergic to everything. Is this . . . creature . . . a gift for little old me?" The sight of her batting her three sets of gloopy eyelashes made Rod feel queasy.

"Indeed it is," confirmed Drobot. "We ask for only one thing in return."

The queen's hideous eyes narrowed.

"And that is?"

"We wish to see the fabled Land Whale," Rod announced, drawing a gasp from the crowd.

"That will not be possible," snapped the

queen. "No one sees the Land Whale but me."

"Probably because it brings folk out in a rash," muttered the king, scratching one of his puny arms.

"Oh," said Lightning Rod, winking at Drobot. "If that is the case, we shall leave immediately. Farewell, people of Tempest Towers."

"Come on, Pop Fizz," added Drobot. "Time to go."

Pop Fizz just roared as he was dragged away.

"No, wait," spluttered the queen. "What about my gift?"

"Let them go, my dumpy darling," wheezed the king, obviously hoping the Skylanders would shut the door on their way out.

"Don't be stupid!" snarled the queen, before forcing a truly terrible smile across her broad face. "They are our honoured guests."

Lightning Rod paused, waiting to see if their ploy would work.

"I'm sure it wouldn't hurt to give them just a

quick peek," the queen simpered, squirming in her throne. "The Land Whale is very pretty after all."

Lightning Rod grinned at Drobot. They were in.

Lightning Rod's smile faltered as soon as the queen led them through her menagerie. The place was as disgusting as the queen herself.

Hundreds of creatures were crammed into the cramped cages that lined the walls of the tower. There were sad-looking unicorns and bearded snakes, warty chompies and winged rhino. A pair of scaled gorillas cowered behind

bars while bored pig-fish swam in aquariums filled with mud. Somewhere, a werewolf howled pitifully, while, in the corner of a rusty cage, a snail the size of a cow sobbed into its own shell.

It was obvious that the queen didn't look after the animals in her zoo. She couldn't even name half the species. All she seemed to care about was that they were hers and no one else's. She stomped ahead, crowing about how secure the place was, how no one could break in, how it was built from the strongest, heaviest stone in all of Skylands.

The king, meanwhile, trailed behind his wife, Pop Fizz's leash in his hand, looking as dejected as the creatures in the cages. Every step brought another royal sneeze, cough or hack. He really was allergic to everything.

"I have never seen such a fine collection," Rod lied, struggling to keep up the pretence. All he wanted to do was fling open the cages and let the animals escape. "You must be very proud."

"Oh, I am," gushed the queen, as they drew near a large tank-like room. "But nothing compares to the jewel in my little zoo's crown."

"You mean the Land Whale?" asked Drobot. "Is it as impressive as the stories say?"

"See for yourself." The queen threw a lever. In front of them, a heavy portcullis squealed as it rose into the ceiling. "Behold, the last of the Land Whales."

She stepped aside, letting Lightning Rod and Drobot walk into the Whale's tank. The Skylanders' mouths dropped open. The Land

Whale was big. Really big. It was roughly the size of four sky-elephants standing side by side – with another four standing on their shoulders.

"How are we going to get it out of this tower?" Drobot hissed quietly. "Are we sure it's even the segment?"

Lightning Rod reached into his belt, drawing out the scrap of paper from the Book of Power.

"The parchment glows so it must be true," he whispered. "But how shall we sneak it past the queen?"

Unfortunately, whispering quietly never was Lightning Rod's strong point.

"I knew it!" came a burbling shout from behind them. "I knew you were trying to steal the whale from me! Well, this is how we deal with thieves around here!"

Before the Skylanders could react, the Cyclops Queen yanked back on the lever and the heavy, iron portcullis came crashing back down, trapping both Lightning Rod and Drobot inside the tank.

Rod rushed forward and tried to lift the barrier, but it was too heavy, even for him.

"I'd save your strength if I were you," the king sniffed, looking as bored as his wife was angry. "No one can lift that thing. You're basically doomed."

"Pah!" boomed Lightning Rod. "It may be heavy, but we can still have a blast, right Drobot?"

"Affirmative," the dragon replied, his eye lasers powering up. Standing side by side, the two Skylanders threw everything they had at the gates, lightning bolts and laser blasts sizzling in the cold air of the tower.

Yet, when the smoke cleared, the gates were still there.

"You'll never escape," crowed the queen. "That's magically reinforced iron – as indestructible as it is heavy. You're trapped, and it serves you right for trying to steal my whale, you rotters! Now, if you don't mind, I'm going to

find your ugly little gift a new home."

"Who you calling little?" snarled Pop Fizz, struggling with the ropes from the balloon. "You wait till I get free of these ropes . . ."

"SIIIILENCE!" the queen bellowed into Pop Fizz's face.

"Woah!" Pop Fizz choked, stunned for a second by the reek of her breath. "Someone needs to floss!"

Before he could continue, cyclopses ran from every corner and threw a glittering net over the berserker.

"Think this can hold me?" yelled Pop Fizz, tearing at the net.

"Actually, it probably can," snorted the king. "Those ropes are woven from bewitched spider-mage webbing. The more you struggle –"

"– the more it tightens!" the queen bellowed, her revolting chin wobbling with laughter. "It's amazing what you can find in my menagerie."

Sure enough, Pop Fizz crashed to the floor,

completely entangled in the net's enchanted embrace. The cyclopses began rolling him away, carefully avoiding his snapping teeth.

"Let us leave the tea-leaves to their fate!" the queen cackled, flouncing after them. The permanently snotty Cyclops King shrugged at the Skylanders.

"It's not all bad, fellas," he wheezed. "At least the Land Whale hasn't woken up . . ."

"What do you mean?" asked Lightning Rod. "Would that be bad?"

"It depends."

"On what?" queried Drobot.

"On whether you think being eaten alive by a giant whale is bad."

With that, the king scurried after his awful wife. "Wait for me, my stout sweet."

Behind the Skylanders, something groaned. Something big.

"Is that what I think it is?" asked Rod.

The sound of huge, gummy lips slapping

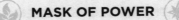 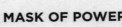

together filled the tank.

The two Skylanders turned slowly round.

The Land Whale had woken up and was glaring at them with eyes the size of doors. Hungry doors.

"Do not fear," droned Drobot nervously. "All evidence suggests the whale is too heavy to move. It will never be able to get to us."

Rod didn't answer. Drobot glanced at his friend and his dragon-heart sank. The Storm Titan's face was emotionless, his eyes glassy. Worst of all, he was slowly stumbling towards the Land Whale.

"What are you doing?" Drobot gasped, but Rod didn't answer. Suddenly it all made sense. The reason the Land Whale had grown so big was that it didn't have to move to catch its food. Its eyes were hypnotic. Its food came to it.

Completely under the creature's thrall, Lightning Rod trudged ever closer to the whale's opening mouth.

CHAPTER TEN

KAOS' GREAT FLOATING HEAD

Outside the city gates, Flynn and Double Trouble watched as Kaos' zeppelin soared towards Tempest Towers.

"So, let me get this right," said Flynn, anxiously playing with his scarf. "The two of us are supposed to stop that thing?"

"Ooga," said Double Trouble.

"By ourselves?"

"Booga!" the spellcaster grinned, waving his staff with glee.

"Thought so," said Flynn, looking more than a little concerned. "Thanks for clearing that up."

High above, Kaos appeared at the prow of the ship and nearly overbalanced, but was caught by Glumshanks at the last minute.

"Glumshanks, you fool! You nearly had me over the edge," Flynn heard the Portal Master squeak. "I was just about to summon my GIANT FLOATING HEAD!"

"Sorry, Lord Kaos," the troll mumbled, looking down in shame as if he'd done something wrong.

Kaos threw up his arms and a massive menacing head manifested itself in mid-air. It was obviously Kaos, but somehow his features looked even more malignant, his expression even more poisonous.

"Ugh," said Flynn. "You can see right up his nose from here."

"People of Tempest Towers!" the head shrieked. "Fear me! Fear KAAAAOOOS!!"

"And he wonders why people don't like him," commented Flynn. "He didn't even say hello.

Didn't his mother teach him any manners?"

"I, KAOS, demand that you bring me the Land Whale right here, right now. Resist me and I will unleash my minions. What's more I will summon the SCARY SHARKBATH OF DEADLY TOOTH-SHARKS! They will swim through your streets, gobbling everything in their path. In short, you will be DOOOOOOOOMED!"

"Yeah, like that's going to work," said Flynn. From behind the thick walls they could hear a lot of scurrying about and excited shouting. "There's no way those cyclopses will just hand over the Land Whale."

High above them, a window opened and the two gatehouse guards poked their heads out, each holding loudhailers in their hands.

"Here we go," sniggered Flynn.

"Kaos, we bring a message from her majesty, the Cyclops Queen," called out Slow Hand.

"He isn't going to like this," Flynn laughed.

"WELL?" shouted Kaos.

"She says that sounds absolutely fine. Please come and pick the whale up from the Royal Menagerie Tower whenever you're ready."

"She said what?" Flynn said, amazed.

"Ooga boo?" Double Trouble said, befuddled.

"WHAAAAAAAT?" roared Kaos. "How dare she defy Kaos? She will rue the day when . . ."

Flynn watched Glumshanks tap the dastardly Portal Master on his bony shoulder and whisper into Kaos' ear.

"Eh?" Kaos said, his Giant Head mimicking his puzzled look. "She agreed to my terms? Just like that? Well, that's . . . a good thing, isn't it!" Kaos turned back to address the city. "Excellent! Thank you, your majesty. A wise decision. Prepare to meet your CONQUEROR!"

Flynn was still scratching his head as the zeppelin thundered over the city walls.

"I just don't get it," said Flynn. "If the queen was happy to just hand over the whale, why

haven't our guys . . . Whoa, what's happening?"

Pop! Pop! Pop! Pop!

The pilot had suddenly found himself lifted off his feet. He looked down to see that Double Trouble had created a bunch of tiny clones that were in the process of picking the two of them up.

"What's the big idea?" Flynn asked.

"Aooga!"

"Nope, still don't a understand a word you're saying, fella. I mean, you could be saying that you're going to detonate these little guys so we're sent flying up over the wall and into the zeppelin, but that would just be nuts, right?"

"Booga ooga!" Double Trouble agreed, nodding sagely.

"Thought as much. So what's the plan?"

Double Trouble giggled madly and blew up the clones anyway.

"WAAAAAAAAAH!" Flynn screamed as they were both propelled up towards the zeppelin.

In the menagerie, Drobot was doing all he could to stop Lightning Rod from walking right into the Land Whale's gaping maw.

He'd tried hauling him back, standing in his path, and even yanking his flowing locks to shock him out of the trance, but it was no good.

Rod was seconds away from becoming whale food.

Time for plan D.

Taking off, Drobot flew towards the creature,

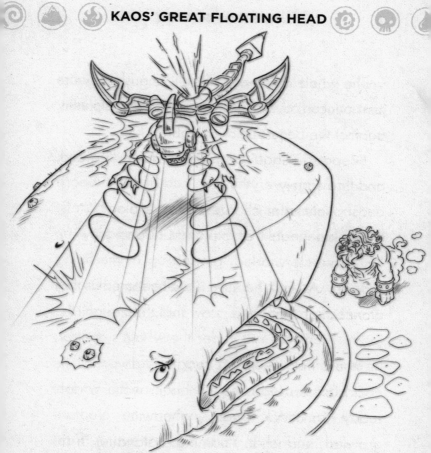

thanking the Portals that his bionic eyes were shielding him from the whale's hypnotic stare. Priming his weapon systems, he unleashed a salvo of galvanized bladegears while simultaneously zapping the gigantic beast with his quadratic blasters.

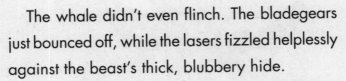
The whale didn't even flinch. The bladegears just bounced off, while the lasers fizzled helplessly against the beast's thick, blubbery hide.

Drobot tried again, swooping around the tank and throwing everything he had at the stubborn beast. Antimatter charges, axon focus crystals, even bladegears that exploded on impact.

The whale snarled, glaring up at the flying dragon. At last he had its attention. Drobot glanced at Rod and saw that, although the Storm Titan was still under the whale's control, he had at least stopped trudging forward.

Drobot soared over the back of the whale, ready to attack again, when the creature growled and shot steaming hot water from the blowhole on its back. The scalding steam blasted into Drobot, smashing him up against the chamber's high stone ceiling.

Winded, Drobot crashed back down to the floor, landing inches away from the whale's slobbering tongue.

CHAPTER ELEVEN

BATTLE!

From their hiding place on the Drow zeppelin, Flynn and Double Trouble watched as the mighty anchor was dropped and the craft came to a halt a few metres from the ground. Everywhere they looked, cyclopses were peering at the ship. They jostled against each other in the streets, hung from balconies and peered over roofs.

Kaos, meanwhile, was enjoying every second of it. Captain Brock lowered the gangplank and the diabolical Portal Master swaggered down to meet the king and queen. The reeking royals were flanked by a pair of snarling creatures known as Slobbering Mutticuses, huge dog-like monsters with serrated teeth and slimy saliva.

"Welcome, oh powerful one," the queen simpered, trying to curtsey but failing miserably.

"Well, it's good to finally be appreciated," Kaos blustered, pug nose held in the air. "Not everyone appreciates my greatness."

"Oh, we do," cooed the queen.

"Do we?" queried the king, looking more than a little bemused by this turn of events.

"Yes," confirmed the queen, through clenched, wonky teeth. "We certainly do."

"Excellent," enthused Kaos. "Then you'll hand over the Land Whale?"

"Oh, must we immediately get down to business?" the queen smirked. "I'd much rather talk about your Giant Floating Head. I've never seen anything quite like it."

Kaos went to smooth the hair on his head, forgetting for a moment that he didn't have any.

"Yes, well, I suppose I am rather unique."

"Thought so!" The grin on the queen's face

reached manic proportions. "Guards! Seize him! I shall add him to my collection!"

"WHAAAAAAT?" bawled Kaos, as he realized he'd just walked into a trap.

On-board the ship, Double Trouble pulled Flynn down behind a stack of barrels.

"Good idea, feathers," Flynn said as they hid from view. "I've got a feeling everything's about to go crazy."

The spellcaster was right. The residents of Tempest Towers, who had been so calmly standing by, suddenly attacked. Cyclops Chuckers pelted the airship with rocks, Armoured Mohawk Warriors whirled their way up the gangplank like axe-wielding tornados, and the Slobbering Mutticuses leapt forward and pinned Kaos and Glumshanks to the ground.

"BROCK!" Kaos brayed, spluttering as he received a faceful of Mutticus slobber. "What are you waiting for? ATTAAAAAAAACK!"

"You heard the boss, boys," Brock yelled.

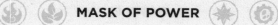

"Let 'em have it!" The Drow moved forward as one, spears and shields raised.

"Boom shaka-laka," Double Trouble insisted, pulling at Flynn's arm.

"Say what?" the pilot squeaked, not taking his eyes off the battle that was raging all around.

The Skylander jabbed forward with his staff. "Booga-booga!"

Flynn looked up and saw Cali tied to the mast.

"Hey, this is our chance to rescue Cali," he exclaimed. "Why didn't you say . . . oh." Flynn's face fell. A Drow Archer had remained on the ship, covering Cali with his bow.

"So what are we gonna do?" Flynn asked. "Send in the clones? Distract him with a little hocus-pocus?"

Double Trouble didn't answer. Instead, he swung his staff around to point at the Drow. Golden beams of crackling Eldritch energy zapped from the staff's glowing orb, hitting the archer in the chest. The Drow lit up like a firework and, a second later, was reduced to a puff of smoke.

Or we could just do that," agreed Flynn as Double Trouble tore across the now empty deck towards Cali.

Drobot shook his head, still dazed from the blast he'd received from the Land Whale's blowhole. He knew he had to do something, but wasn't sure what it was.

Then, just as the whale's gigantic, slobbery tongue tried to flip him into its open mouth, Drobot remembered.

He needed to get away from that open mouth.

But it was too late. Drobot landed with a splat in the whale's mouth and was immediately stuck fast to the sticky saliva that coated its tongue.

"Lightning Rod!" Drobot bellowed. "Get me out of here!"

Rod, still in a trance, stared stupidly at the whale. Someone was calling his name, someone he knew. But that didn't matter. All he wanted to do was feed the whale, to step into the creature's mouth and slide down to its wonderfully welcoming stomach.

"Rod! Please!"

But . . . wasn't that Drobot? His friend? And didn't it sound like Drobot was in danger?

Drobot! In danger!

The thought snapped Rod back to his senses. Whatever had he been thinking? His eyes grew wide as he saw Drobot clambering around on the whale's tacky tongue.

"What are you doing in there?" he asked, a lightning harpoon instinctively forming in his clenched fist.

"Trying not to be swallowed!" came the reply. Rod had never heard Drobot sound so frantic.

"You dare to eat my friend?" Rod shouted, throwing the bolt into the whale's face at point-blank range. "One strike and you're out!"

The bolt exploded and the beast roared,

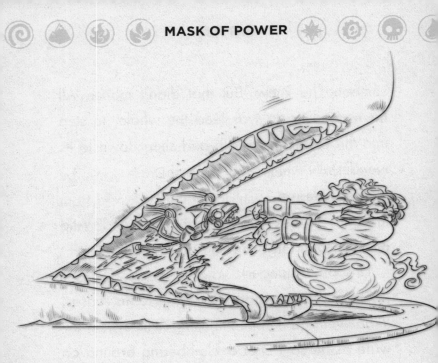

giving Rod the chance to reach in, grab Drobot's
front claws and heave as hard as he could.

With a sickening squelch, Drobot came
unstuck and the two Skylanders rolled away
from the thrashing whale.

"Thank you," gasped Drobot, shaking
stinking whale spit from his mechanical wings.

"Do not thank me yet," Lightning Rod insisted.
"We still need to escape this tank!

"Hey, Cali," Flynn said, popping up behind the tied-up explorer. "Miss me?"

"You have no idea how much," Cali said, never taking her eyes off the Drow who, by now, had pretty much driven the cyclopses from the ship. Every single Drow was busy in battle, their hostage forgotten. "Just untie me, OK?"

"So you can throw yourself into my arms?" Flynn started struggling with the ropes. "It's understandable. I feel the same way too."

Then the pilot frowned.

"Hmmm. Who knew the Drow were so good at tying knots?"

Double Trouble shoved Flynn aside. "Booga ooga!"

A flash of Eldritch energy blasted the rope and it unravelled, landing at Cali's feet.

"So, what about that hug?" said Flynn, throwing his arms wide.

"How about you tell me the next stage of your amazing rescue plan?" Cali shot back.

"Oh, that." Flynn put his hands on his hips and puffed out his chest. "It's simple. We're just going to, um . . ."

Cali folded her arms and raised an eyebrow.

"And then we're going to, er . . ."

"Booga? Pssh-booga!" interrupted Double Trouble.

"Oh, I know," said Cali. "He hasn't a clue."

"Wait a minute," Flynn's eyebrows shot up. "You mean you can understand him?"

"Of course," said Cali. "And I thought you could fly anything."

"I can!" replied Flynn, indignantly.

"Anything, like a Drow zeppelin for instance?"

The grin slowly returned to Flynn's face. Now they were talking.

CHAPTER **TWELVE**

BAITING THE BEAST

As the Land Whale writhed around behind them, Lightning Rod made one last attempt to raise the portcullis, but it was hopeless.

"Wait," said Drobot, as excitedly as his robotic tones ever got. "Look over there."

Rod did as he was told, and saw Pop Fizz trapped in what looked like an oversized stone birdcage on the other side of the corridor. Amazingly, he was still in his beast form. He must have drunk a lot of potion to still be big and furry after all this time.

"Fizz!" he called over. "You need to get over

here and get us out!"

"No, no, no," the alchemist jibbered, making a show of attempting to bend the stone bars. "See, see, see?"

"The cage is made of Cyclopnite," said Drobot. "He'll never be able to break out."

"And he is too large to slip through the gaps," Rod noted.

"Slip through the gaps," repeated Pop Fizz, excitedly. "Yeah, yeah, yeah. Gaps!"

As Rod and Drobot looked on in bemusement, Pop Fizz started somersaulting round and round the cage."

"He's gone mad," Drobot said, confused.

"No, he has not," boomed Rod, realizing what Pop Fizz was doing. "Use that amazing brain of yours, dragon. The more excited Pop Fizz becomes, the faster he uses up his potion and the sooner . . ."

" . . . he will return to his normal size," Drobot finished, smiling.

Pop Fizz was now tumbling round the cage so fast that he looked like a blur of fur, teeth and claws. Rod and Drobot cheered him on until . . .

POP!

He was back to normal. The potion had completely worn off. The alchemist staggered slightly, still a bit dizzy, before squeezing through the stone bars.

It was still a bit tight, but he managed to push himself between them and drop down to the flagstones.

"Well done, courageous alchemist!" applauded Lightning Rod. "Now throw the lever and release us."

Pop Fizz charged across to the tank and pushed the lever, sending the portcullis creaking up into the ceiling.

They were free!

Of course, there was still one problem.

"So, how are we going to get the Land Whale out of this place?" asked Pop Fizz.

Outside, the battle wasn't going to plan for the cyclopses. It had started well. They'd had the element of surprise on their side, for one thing. For another, there were an awful lot of them. The only snag was, when it came to battles, Drow were simply better fighters. Cyclops Spinners, for example, whizz into the fray, axes flashing, but soon get so dizzy that they can hardly stand up. Drow Spearmen, on the other hand, barely even stop for breath when attacking and never once lose their balance. Cyclops Chuckers and Timidclopses, meanwhile, are great at throwing bombs and rolling barrels at their foes, but both are as lily-livered as you can get.

Even the Slobbering Mutticuses may look fierce, but this time they had picked the wrong Portal Master to pounce on.

From beneath Mutticus paws, Kaos shrieked, not in pain but in anger.

"How dare you attack KAOS!" he screamed. "I summon the TERRIBLE TWIRLING

DOOMTWISTERS . . . OF DOOOOOOOM!"

The air around the square seemed to darken as terrifying tornadoes swept in from every corner. One by one, the cyclops warriors were plucked from their feet and pulled helplessly into the swirling maelstroms. In the middle stood Kaos, arms outstretched, cackling at the top of his lungs. With another wave of his hands, the tornadoes vanished, along with the cyclopses they had hoovered up. Those who had escaped the doomtwisters simply turned and fled, leaving the square deserted.

The Cyclops King wanted to run, but couldn't because a Drow Witch had turned him into a potted plant. A petunia, to be precise. The queen, unfortunately, hadn't been turned into anything, and looked as hideous as ever. She had, however, been tied to a lamppost by Brock. The green brute had always been proud of his knots, ever since he'd been a member of the Goliath Drow Scouts as a young lad. The

Drow Scouts' motto? Always Be Prepared . . . to Punch Anything That Moves.

Looking eminently pleased with himself, Kaos wiped dust from his sleeve and peered evilly at the tied-up tyrant.

"Now, where were we?" Kaos crowed. "Oh yes, I remember. WHERE IS MY WHALE?"

The queen glared at Kaos, hatred simmering in all three of her eyes.

"I think you mean MY whale!" she snarled back. "He's behind those doors back there." She indicated the massive stone doors that led into the menagerie. "But they only open when you say the password."

"And that password is?"

"For me to know and you to NEVER find out!"

Everyone prepared for another outburst, but instead Kaos' gaze fell on the potted plant by his feet. A potted plant that seemed to be shaking with fright. Kaos chuckled.

"Glumshanks," he said softly. "Is that plant

who I think it is?"

"His one-eyed majesty," confirmed the troll.

In one fluid movement, the Portal Master snatched up the petunia and raised it high above his head.

"Tell me the password or I WILL SMASH THIS PLANT INTO A MILLION LITTLE PIECES."

"Smash it then!" roared the queen. "I will never reveal the password!"

"I will," came a tiny little voice. "I'll tell you the password. Just don't smash me!"

Kaos looked at the plant and laughed a wicked laugh. "Nothing can stop me now!" he cawed. "The Air segment will be mine, MINE, MIIIIIIIIINE!"

CHAPTER **THIRTEEN**

ROD WORKS IT OUT

High in the tower, Drobot was watching the scene unfold.

"Kaos is going to open the door," he reported. "I estimate we have three minutes and forty-two seconds before this tower is swarming with Drow."

When no one replied, the dragon turned round and sighed. Pop Fizz seemed oblivious to the imminent danger and was hopping about, ogling the animals behind the bars. He looked as excited as a troll in a dynamite factory.

Rod, on the other hand, was staring at the

scrap of glowing paper in his hand, deep in thought.

"Did you not hear? Kaos is on his way – OW!"

Something clanged off Drobot's helmet. He span round as another tiny missile whizzed towards him. He watched it land on the ground next to him. A Drow coin. But who was throwing them?

He peered out of the window and a smile spread over his face. Down below, all eyes were on Kaos. They hadn't noticed Double Trouble raise the Drow zeppelin's anchor with a blast of Eldritch energy, hadn't spotted Flynn take the wheel, hadn't even twigged that the airship was rising slowly to the tower window. On the deck, Cali was just about to chuck another coin but, when she saw she had Drobot's attention, she waved happily.

"Rod," said Drobot. "We could use the zeppelin to transport the whale."

But Rod still wasn't listening. Instead, he

was pressing the paper against the tower wall, watching as it flared even more brightly.

"Rod! What are you doing?"

Finally, the Storm Titan turned to face the dragon, an urgent look in his eyes.

"Silence!" he boomed. "I know what we need to do!"

In the square, Kaos was still laughing manically.

"All power will be mine. Bwa-ha-ha-HAAAAAA!"

"Er, Lord Kaos," said Glumshanks, already cringing from the rebuke he was sure to receive. "Shouldn't we celebrate after we've been told the password and entered the tower?"

"WHAAAAAT?" screamed Kaos. "Can't an evil Portal Master savour his moment of victory?"

"Milk it more like," said the queen.

Flashing her a vicious look, Kaos snapped his fingers and the pot plant became the wimpy king again.

"Tell me the password," Kaos sneered, obviously enjoying the fact that he could tower over someone for once. "Tell me the password now, or I will . . ."

"Pipsqueak," said the king.

"WHAAAAT DID YOU CALL MEEEEEE?!?" yelled Kaos, incensed.

"No, you don't understand," the king sniffed. "The password is Pipsqueak . . . my name."

"Oh," Kaos said, instantly regaining his composure. "That's different then. So all I have to do is . . ."

". . . say the magic word and the doors to the menagerie will open."

"No point," said Glumshanks, looking over Kaos' shoulder.

"What do you mean 'no point', you ignoramus?" shrieked Kaos. "Of course there's a point! Ultimate power is the point."

"Yes, Lord Kaos, but I meant that there's no point as the doors are already open."

Kaos span round and gasped. The doors had opened a crack and someone was popping his head through the gap. That someone was Pop Fizz.

"You might want to look up," said Pop Fizz, before flashing a winning smile and slamming the doors shut once again.

For once, Kaos did what he was told, and saw Lightning Rod hanging out of the window.

"Hello, little man," the Storm Titan bellowed. "You desire the Land Whale, do you not?"

"It's mine!" Kaos screamed back. "And you won't stop me taking it."

"Excellent," Rod shouted back. "If you want the whale, you shall have the whale."

"What do you mean, he can have it?" spluttered Drobot. The dragon couldn't believe

135

what the Storm Titan was doing. Rod had rushed into the Land Whale's tank and, with supreme effort, had somehow managed to pull the still-dazed creature out of its chamber.

"None of this computes."

Lightning Rod didn't reply. Amazingly, unbelievably, he strained against the weight of the whale and began to swing the beast round by its tail. Moving slowly at first, it soon built up speed, spinning like the hammer he'd thrown at the Storm Games.

"Get . . . away . . . from . . . the . . . window," Rod growled as he whizzed round, the whale becoming a big grey blur. Drobot scampered out of the way and, when he was clear, Rod let go.

The whale shot forward. It was far too big to pass through the window, so it just smashed through the wall. As Drobot watched, the beast soared through the air, narrowly missing the zeppelin, and heading out towards the Sea of Storms.

CHAPTER FOURTEEN

FOLLOW THAT WHALE

"**B**rock didn't know whales could fly," said Brock, dumbstruck by the sight of the blubbering beast zipping through the air high above.

"MY WHALE!" screamed Kaos and the queen in unison.

It had already almost disappeared from view.

"What has that fool done?" shouted Kaos, not knowing whether to rant or cry. "We need to get after it. BACK TO THE SHIP!"

"That may be a problem!" gulped Glumshanks, pointing at the stolen zeppelin that was now moored by the gaping hole in the side of the tower.

Kaos' face turned a particularly nasty shade of purple.

"Gah! We'll just have to travel by foot then. Brock, carry me." The Goliath Drow obediently hoisted the Portal Master, none too graciously, over his shoulder.

"The rest of you," Kaos continued, so intent on his prize that he forgave the indignity for a moment. "FOLLOW THAT WHALE!"

As the Drow rushed from the city, Flynn threw a rope from the zeppelin over to the tower.

"How about some warning next time you're chucking whales around, big guy?" the pilot suggested to Lightning Rod. "You nearly took out our crow's nest."

"I still do not understand," Drobot whirred, his face a picture of confusion. "You just threw away the Air segment."

"No, I didn't," insisted Rod, producing the scrap of paper from his belt. It was still glowing, brighter than ever. "It was not the Land Whale that was making the parchment of power glow. Behold!" He slapped it against the wall and the light intensified.

"It was the tower!" said Drobot, the penny finally dropping.

"Made of Cyclopnite, the heaviest stone ever

mined," Rod reminded him. "This tower is the heaviest thing on Skylands."

"So Kaos . . ."

". . . is on a whale of a wild goose chase!"

"Ooga!" exclaimed Double Trouble, waving his staff and spinning into a victory chant.

"But how are we supposed to get an entire tower back to the archive?" asked Cali.

"I think I can help with that," said a voice from behind them. Rod turned to see Pop Fizz brandishing a bottle. The Storm Titan looked suspiciously at the murky liquid sloshing around inside.

"What is that, alchemist?"

"Oh, just a little brew I've concocted from some of the animals in this place. They're amazing. Some of the rarest and most potent creatures in all of Skylands. All it needed was some rhino feathers, a splash of pig-fish milk, a little cow-snail slime and a few scales from those nice gorillas back there. As the queen said, it's amazing what you can find in the menagerie!"

Lightning Rod grimaced.

"And you mean to drink such a disgusting brew?"

Pop Fizz laughed. "Of course I'm not going to drink it."

Rod let out a sigh of relief, but it was short-lived.

Pop Fizz grinned a knowing grin. "You are!"

"What are you doing?" squealed the Cyclops Queen as her minions pulled at Brock's expert knots.

"They're trying to release you, my sickly sweet," simpered the king.

"Forget about me!" the queen screamed. "GET THOSE SKYLANDERS OUT OF MY TOWER!"

"You heard the woman," the king commanded, before realizing that all their guards had either been magicked away or fled. "You just can't

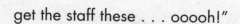

get the staff these . . . ooooh!"

Beneath their feet, the ground shuddered.

"Just when I thought today couldn't get any worse," whinged the queen, "we have an earthquake."

"I think it may be more than just an earthquake, my dumpy darling," admitted the king, noticing the cloud that had started to spread out from under the tower doors. "I think we've got a bigger problem."

And bigger it was. The menagerie tower was lifted into the air by a huge, massive, ginormous figure: Lightning Rod.

"I take it all back," he bellowed, his voice the volume of a thousand thunderstorms. "That potion was delicious. True ambrosia of the ancients!"

High above, Pop Fizz was hanging from the gaping hole in the side of the tower. "And it did the trick too. One supersized Storm Titan ready to go!"

"Let's get this tower back to the archive," Drobot called down.

"Booga booga boo!" yelled Double Trouble.

If a normal-sized Lightning Rod was strong, a humongous Lightning Rod was a hundred times stronger. As the queen sobbed, Rod hefted the tower high into the sky and away from the city, the Drow zeppelin soaring close behind.

"My beautiful collection!" she wailed. "Gone forever!"

"Well, at least I won't sneeze any more," remarked the king, smiling for the first time anyone could remember. "For every cloud, there's a silver lining . . ."

CHAPTER FIFTEEN
THE AIR ELEMENT

Back at the Eternal Archive, Pop Fizz was coaxing a scaled gorilla on to the Portal of Power. When it was in the centre of the raised platform, Eon waved his hand and the creature vanished, sent back to where it belonged.

"That is that," announced Drobot. "Every specimen from the queen's collection has been sent home. Mission accomplished."

"Not quite," said Cali. "We still have THAT thing to deal with."

She was pointing up at the great stone tower that was still standing where Lightning Rod had dropped it – beside the walls of the Eternal Archive.

"Allow me," said Eon, raising his arms once again and closing his eyes. Standing beside Cali, the now normal-sized Rod felt his beard tingle as the air itself seemed to crackle with energy. The menagerie tower was bathed in brilliant white light, so bright that the Skylanders had to shield their eyes. When they finally looked again, the building had been replaced by a tiny wooden fragment that floated down to Eon's open palm.

"The Air segment is safe," Eon announced proudly. "Well done, my Skylanders."

"Hey, it was nothing," said Flynn.

"Nothing?" repeated Drobot, not sure he was hearing this right.

"OK, OK, I admit it," laughed Flynn, raising his hands. "It was amazing. My trouble is that I'm too modest."

"You were all amazing," said Rod, gathering

his friends into a massive bear hug. For once, the Storm Titan didn't want to hog all the limelight. "I could not have completed the quest without you."

"I don't know," giggled Cali. "You looked like a pretty big hero to me!"

Eon smiled as he watched his Skylanders celebrate, but his expression faltered as he looked down at the fragment of the Mask in his hand. There was one thing that he still didn't understand. How had Kaos known where the segment was hidden? It made no sense. He sighed sadly. The mystery would have to wait for another day. In the meantime, the Air fragment needed to be stored safely in the vault.

"Squirmgrub?" Eon called, looking around for the Warrior Librarian. "Could you take this down to . . ."

But Squirmgrub was nowhere to be seen.

In a secret chamber, deep in the bowels of the Eternal Archive, the Warrior Librarian Squirmgrub carried a small wooden box to a table. Placing it down, he opened the lid and carefully lifted a crystal ball from inside.

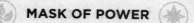
Nestled in his robotic hands, the crystal began to glow, smoke swirling inside the glass. The uncanny mist twisted and turned before parting to reveal a face – a particularly nasty face.

"Well?" snapped Kaos from within the communication crystal.

"My Lord," Squirmgrub whispered, not wanting to be overheard. "The Skylanders have the Air fragment."

"I know that, fool. I realized that whale wasn't the segment as soon as it ATE HALF MY DROW!" the Portal Master snapped. "But never mind that. What about the next fragment? The Earth fragment?"

Squirmgrub shook his heavy, mechanical head.

"The Book of Power has yet to reveal its location," he said. "But when it does . . ."

"You will tell me immediately," Kaos commanded, a wicked grin flickering over his cruel lips. "Like the good little traitor you are . . ."

The sound of Kaos' demented laughter echoed around the chamber.

ONK BEAKMAN

TERRAFIN

BATTLES THE
BOOM BROTHERS

CHAPTER ONE

PROFESSOR PUCK'S FANTASTIC FAIR

"Roll up, roll up! Professor Puck's Fantastic Fair is in town. You will be amazed. You will be astonished. You won't believe your eyes!"

Gurglefin the Gillman rubbed his webbed hands together with glee. He'd been waiting for this moment all year. Professor Puck's fair was famous throughout Skylands. Everyone knew about it. The crazy games, the fin-raising rides, the strange sights. And the delicious smells. Oh, the smells! Doughnuts, popcorn and pretzels, toffee apples, candyfloss and gingerbread. His mouth was watering at the very thought.

The only problem was what to try first. Everywhere he turned, Gurglefin was presented with fresh treats and new opportunities for fun and excitement. Lights flashed, music played and carny folk called out, trying to entice him to their various stalls.

Then something caught his eye. There, behind the helter-skelter and the Hook-a-Chompy, stood a small, modest-looking red tent, with a hand-painted sign hung over its dark entrance.

MADAME DESTINY:
FORTUNES TOLD
FUTURES PREDICTED

Yes, thought Gurglefin. That's the place to start. Madame Destiny can tell me what I'd enjoy most.

He waddled over excitedly, silver coins at the ready with which to cross Madame Destiny's palm. There she was, hunched over a crystal ball in the mouth of the tent. She was wearing a dark, crimson scarf round her head and a pink, sequined veil across her face. As he drew nearer, Gurglefin slowed. There was something sinister about the old woman; something not quite right. Maybe it was her piercing red eyes or the stubby fingers that she waved above the crystal.

Or maybe it was her pong. Phew! Did she ever reek!

But, after coming this far, Gurglefin was in no mood to be a scaredy-catfish. This was just a harmless bit of fun; a harmless old woman. Nothing to be afraid of at all.

He crept nearer the stall and cleared his throat.

"Er, h-hello," he croaked. "Madame Destiny?"

The old hag didn't look up. He tried again.

"Madame Destiny, I was wondering if you could –"

"What do you want?" the woman snapped,

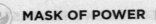
throwing her arms round the crystal as if trying to hide it from view.

"J-just to have my fortune told," stammered Gurglefin.

"And why should I do that?" she shrieked.

"Er, because you're a fortune teller?" he suggested, holding out two coins in a shaking hand.

The old woman growled, looked at the coins and then looked at Gurglefin. Without warning, she shot out a hand, snaffled the coins away and snapped at the nervy Gillman.

"You want to know what the future holds?" she barked, fixing him with a wicked glare.

Gurglefin just nodded, wondering if he really did.

"Are you sure?" she teased, her veil shifting as if she was smiling underneath.

"I g-guess so . . ."

"Then I predict you will come to a STICKY

END!" Madame Destiny screamed. "NOW, SLING YER HOOK, FISHFACE!"

Who is the mysterious (and downright grouchy) Madame Destiny?

Why is sweet stuff exploding?

And can Terrafin find the Earth segment of the Mask of Power?

Find out all this and more in . . .

TERRAFIN
BATTLES THE BOOM BROTHERS

HEAD TO HEAD

Which Skylander do you like best - the powerful Storm Titan or the hi-tech robo-dragon?

LIGHTNING ROD

ROUND 1: ORIGINS

For centuries, Lightning Rod dominated the Storm Titan Games. Then, Kaos decided to invade the Cloud Kingdom. Outraged, Rod threw a lightning bolt through the evil Portal Master's floating head, where it proceeded to electrocute Kaos in his hidden airship. Rod's bravery hadn't gone unnoticed. Master Eon immediately made the bearded legend a Skylander.

ROUND 2: BATTLE CRY

One Strike and You're Out!

ROUND 3: PERSONALITY

Rod can be a little self-centred, mainly due to the fact that he has so many fans. But, as his autobiography – 'Rod the Bod' – testifies, he is also heroic and brave.

ROUND 4: WEAPONS

Rod's lightning bolts always leave leave enemies feeling under the weather.

ROUND 5: SPECIAL ABILITIES

When things get stormy, Lightning Rod can summon zapper clouds to thunder down on enemies.

TOTAL: